THE HORROR AT RED HOOK

Start Publishing PD LLC

Manufactured in the United States of America

Cover art: Shutterstock/Taisiya Kozorez

Cover design: Jennifer Do

10 9 8 7 6 5 4 3 2 1

ISBN 979-8-8809-1649-8

THE HORROR AT RED HOOK

by H. P. Lovecraft

TABLE OF CONTENTS

I

Not many weeks ago, on a street corner in the village of Pascoag, Rhode Island, a tall, heavily built, and wholesome-looking pedestrian furnished much speculation by a singular lapse of behaviour. He had, it appears, been descending the hill by the road from Chepachet; and encountering the compact section, had turned to his left into the main thoroughfare where several modest business blocks convey a touch of the urban. At this point, without visible provocation, he committed his astonishing lapse; staring queerly for a second at the tallest of the buildings before him, and then, with a series of terrified, hysterical shrieks, breaking into a frantic run which ended in a stumble and fall at the next crossing. Picked up and dusted off by ready hands, he was found to be conscious, organically unhurt, and evidently cured of his sudden nervous attack. He muttered some shamefaced explanations involving a strain he had undergone, and with downcast glance turned back up the Chepachet road, trudging out of sight without once looking behind him. It was a strange incident to befall so large, robust, normal-featured, and capable-looking a man, and the strangeness was not lessened by the remarks of a bystander who had recognised him as the boarder of a well-known dairyman on the outskirts of Chepachet.

He was, it developed, a New York police detective named Thomas F. Malone, now on a long leave of absence under medical treatment after some disproportionately arduous work on a gruesome local case which accident had made dramatic. There had been a collapse of several old brick buildings during a raid in which he had shared, and something about the wholesale loss of life, both of prisoners and of his companions, had peculiarly appalled him. As a result, he had acquired an acute and anomalous horror of any buildings even remotely suggesting the ones which had fallen in, so that in the end mental specialists forbade him the sight of such things for an indefinite period. A police surgeon with relatives in Chepachet had put forward that quaint hamlet of wooden colonial houses as an ideal spot for the psychological convalescence; and thither the sufferer had gone, promising never to venture among the brick-lined streets of larger villages till duly advised by the Woonsocket specialist with whom he was put in touch. This walk to Pascoag for magazines had been a mistake, and the patient had paid in fright, bruises, and humiliation for his disobedience.

So much the gossips of Chepachet and Pascoag knew; and so much, also, the most learned specialists believed. But Malone had at first told the specialists much more, ceasing only when he saw that utter incredulity was his portion. Thereafter he held his peace, protesting not at all when it was generally agreed that the collapse of certain squalid brick houses in the Red Hook section of Brooklyn, and the consequent death of many brave officers, had unseated his nervous equilibrium. He had worked too hard, all said, in trying to clean up those nests of disorder and violence; certain features were shocking enough, in all conscience, and the unexpected tragedy was the last straw. This was a simple explanation which everyone could understand, and because Malone was not a simple person he perceived that he had better let it suffice. To hint to unimaginative people of a horror beyond all human conception—a horror of houses and blocks and cities leprous and cancerous with evil dragged from elder worlds—would be merely to invite a padded cell instead of a restful rustication, and Malone was a man of sense despite his mysticism. He had the Celt's far vision of weird and hidden things, but the logician's quick eye for the outwardly unconvincing; an amalgam which had led him far afield in the forty-two years of his life, and set him in strange places for a Dublin University man born in a Georgian villa near Phoenix Park.

And now, as he reviewed the things he had seen and felt and apprehended, Malone was content to keep unshared the secret of what could reduce a dauntless fighter to a quivering neurotic; what could make old brick slums and seas of dark, subtle faces a thing of nightmare and eldritch portent. It would not be the first time his sensations had been forced to bide uninterpreted—for was not his very act of plunging into the polyglot abyss of New York's underworld a freak beyond sensible explanation? What could he tell the prosaic of the antique witcheries and grotesque marvels discernible to sensitive eyes amidst the poison cauldron where all the varied dregs of unwholesome ages mix their venom and perpetuate their obscene terrors? He had seen the hellish green flame of secret wonder in this blatant, evasive welter of outward greed and inward blasphemy, and had smiled gently when all the New-Yorkers he knew scoffed at his experiment in police work. They had been very witty and cynical, deriding his fantastic pursuit of unknowable mysteries and assuring him that in these days New York held nothing but cheapness and vulgarity. One of them had wagered him a heavy sum that he could not—despite many poignant things to his credit in the Dublin Review—even write a truly interesting story of New York low life; and now, looking back, he perceived that cosmic irony had justified the prophet's words while secretly confuting their flippant meaning. The horror, as glimpsed at last, could not make a story—for like the book cited by Poe's German authority, 'es lässt sich nicht lesen—it does not permit itself to be read.'

II

To Malone the sense of latent mystery in existence was always present. In youth he had felt the hidden beauty and ecstasy of things, and had been a poet; but poverty and sorrow and exile had turned his gaze in darker directions, and he had thrilled at the imputations of evil in the world around. Daily life had for him come to be a phantasmagoria of macabre shadow-studies; now glittering and leering with concealed rottenness as in Beardsley's best manner, now hinting terrors behind the commonest shapes and objects as in the subtler and less obvious work of Gustave Doré. He would often regard it as merciful that most persons of high intelligence jeer at the inmost mysteries; for, he argued, if superior minds were ever placed in fullest contact with the secrets preserved by ancient and lowly cults, the resultant abnormalities would soon not only wreck the world, but threaten the very integrity of the universe. All this reflection was no doubt morbid, but keen logic and a deep sense of humour ably offset it. Malone was satisfied to let his notions remain as half-spied and forbidden visions to be lightly played with; and hysteria came only when duty flung him into a hell of revelation too sudden and insidious to escape.

He had for some time been detailed to the Butler Street station in Brooklyn when the Red Hook matter came to his notice. Red Hook is a maze of hybrid squalor near the ancient waterfront opposite Governor's Island, with dirty highways climbing the hill from the wharves to that higher ground where the decayed lengths of Clinton and Court Streets lead off toward the Borough Hall. Its houses are mostly of brick, dating from the first quarter to the middle of the nineteenth century, and some of the obscurer alleys and byways have that alluring antique flavour which conventional reading leads us to call 'Dickensian'. The population is a hopeless tangle and enigma; Syrian, Spanish, Italian, and Negro elements impinging upon one another, and fragments of Scandinavian and American belts lying not far distant. It is a babel of sound and filth, and sends out strange cries to answer the lapping oily waves at its grimy piers and the monstrous organ litanies of the harbour whistles. Here long ago a brighter picture dwelt, with clear—eyed mariners on the lower streets and homes of taste and substance where the larger houses line the hill. One can trace the relics of this former happiness in the trim shapes of the buildings, the occasional graceful churches, and the evidences of original art and background in bits of detail here and there—a worn flight of steps, a battered doorway, a wormy pair of decorative columns or pilasters, or a fragment of once green space with bent and rusted iron railing. The houses are generally in solid blocks, and now and then a many-windowed cupola arises to tell of days when the households of captains and ship-owners watched the sea.

From this tangle of material and spiritual putrescence the blasphemies of an hundred dialects assail the sky. Hordes of prowlers reel shouting and singing along the lanes and thoroughfares, occasional furtive hands suddenly extinguish lights and pull down curtains, and swarthy, sin-pitted faces disappear from windows when visitors pick their way through. Policemen despair of order or reform, and seek rather to erect barriers protecting the outside world from the contagion. The clang of the patrol is answered by a kind of spectral silence, and such prisoners as are taken are never communicative. Visible offences are as varied as the local dialects, and run the gamut from the smuggling of rum and prohibited aliens through diverse stages of lawlessness and obscure vice to murder and mutilation in their most abhorrent guises. That these visible affairs are not more frequent is not to the neighbourhood's credit, unless the power of concealment be an art demanding credit. More people enter Red Hook than leave it—or at least, than leave it by the landward side—and those who are not loquacious are the likeliest to leave.

Malone found in this state of things a faint stench of secrets more terrible than any of the sins denounced by citizens and bemoaned by priests and philanthropists. He was conscious, as one who united imagination with scientific knowledge, that modern people under lawless conditions tend uncannily to repeat the darkest instinctive patterns of primitive half-ape savagery in their daily life and ritual observances; and he had often viewed with an anthropologist's shudder the chanting, cursing processions of blear-eyed and pockmarked young men which wound their way along in the dark small hours of morning. One saw groups of these youths incessantly; sometimes in leering vigils on street corners, sometimes in doorways playing eerily on cheap instruments of music, sometimes in stupefied dozes or indecent dialogues around cafeteria tables near Borough Hall, and sometimes in whispering converse around dingy taxicabs drawn up at the high stoops of crumbling and closely shuttered old houses. They chilled and fascinated him more than he dared confess to his associates on the force, for he seemed to see in them some monstrous thread of secret continuity; some fiendish, cryptical, and ancient pattern utterly beyond and below the sordid mass of facts and habits and haunts listed with such conscientious technical care by the police. They must be, he felt inwardly, the heirs of some shocking and primordial tradition; the sharers of debased and broken scraps from cults and ceremonies older than mankind. Their coherence and definiteness suggested it, and it shewed in the singular suspicion of order which lurked beneath their squalid disorder. He had not read in vain such treatises as Miss Murray's Witch-Cult in Western Europe; and knew that up to recent years there had certainly survived among peasants and furtive folk a frightful and clandestine system of assemblies and orgies descended from dark religions antedating the Aryan world, and appearing in popular legends as Black Masses and Witches' Sabbaths. That these hellish vestiges of old Turanian-Asiatic magic and fertility cults were even now wholly dead he could not for a moment suppose, and he frequently wondered how much older and how much blacker than the very worst of the muttered tales some of them might really be.

III

It was the case of Robert Suydam which took Malone to the heart of things in Red Hook. Suydam was a lettered recluse of ancient Dutch family, possessed originally of barely independent means, and inhabiting the spacious but ill-preserved mansion which his grandfather had built in Flatbush when that village was little more than a pleasant group of colonial cottages surrounding the steepled and ivy-clad Reformed Church with its iron-railed yard of Netherlandish gravestones. In his lonely house, set back from Martense Street amidst a yard of venerable trees, Suydam had read and brooded for some six decades except for a period a generation before, when he had sailed for the old world and remained there out of sight for eight years. He could afford no servants, and would admit but few visitors to his absolute solitude; eschewing close friendships and receiving his rare acquaintances in one of the three ground-floor rooms which he kept in order—a vast, high-ceiled library whose walls were solidly packed with tattered books of ponderous, archaic, and vaguely repellent aspect. The growth of the town and its final absorption in the Brooklyn district had meant nothing to Suydam, and he had come to mean less and less to the town. Elderly people still pointed him out on the streets, but to most of the recent population he was merely a queer, corpulent old fellow whose unkempt white hair, stubbly beard, shiny black clothes, and gold-headed cane earned him an amused glance and nothing more. Malone did not know him by sight till duty called him to the case, but had heard of him indirectly as a really profound authority on mediaeval superstition, and had once idly meant to look up an out-of-print pamphlet of his on the

Kabbalah and the Faustus legend, which a friend had quoted from memory.

Suydam became a case when his distant and only relatives sought court pronouncements on his sanity. Their action seemed sudden to the outside world, but was really undertaken only after prolonged observation and sorrowful debate. It was based on certain odd changes in his speech and habits; wild references to impending wonders, and unaccountable hauntings of disreputable Brooklyn neighbourhoods. He had been growing shabbier and shabbier with the years, and now prowled about like a veritable mendicant; seen occasionally by humiliated friends in subway stations, or loitering on the benches around Borough Hall in conversation with groups of swarthy, evil-looking strangers. When he spoke it was to babble of unlimited powers almost within his grasp, and to repeat with knowing leers such mystical words or names as 'Sephiroth', 'Ashmodai', and 'Samaël'. The court action revealed that he was using up his income and wasting his principal in the purchase of curious tomes imported from London and Paris, and in the maintenance of a squalid basement flat in the Red Hook district where he spent nearly every night, receiving odd delegations of mixed rowdies and foreigners, and apparently conducting some kind of ceremonial service behind the green blinds of secretive windows. Detectives assigned to follow him reported strange cries and chants and prancing of feet filtering out from these nocturnal rites, and shuddered at their peculiar ecstasy and abandon despite the commonness of weird orgies in that sodden section. When, however, the matter came to a hearing, Suydam managed to preserve his liberty. Before the judge his manner grew urbane and reasonable, and he freely admitted the queerness of demeanour and extravagant cast of language into which he had fallen through excessive devotion to study and research. He was, he said, engaged in the investigation of certain details of European tradition which required the closest contact with foreign groups and their songs and folk dances. The notion that any low secret society was preying upon him, as hinted by his relatives, was obviously absurd; and shewed how sadly limited was their understanding of him and his work. Triumphing with his calm explanations, he was suffered to depart unhindered; and the paid detectives of the Suydams, Corlears, and Van Brunts were withdrawn in resigned disgust.

It was here that an alliance of Federal inspectors and police, Malone with them, entered the case. The law had watched the Suydam action with interest, and had in many instances been called upon to aid the private detectives. In this work it developed that Suydam's new associates were among the blackest and most vicious criminals of Red Hook's devious lanes, and that at least a third of them were known and repeated offenders in the matter of thievery, disorder, and the importation of illegal immigrants. Indeed, it would not have been too much to say that the old scholar's particular circle coincided almost perfectly with the worst of the organized cliques which smuggled ashore certain nameless and unclassified Asian dregs wisely turned back by Ellis Island. In the teeming rookeries of Parker Place—since renamed—where Suydam had his basement flat, there had grown up a very unusual colony of unclassified slant-eyed folk who used the Arabic alphabet but were eloquently repudiated by the great mass of Syrians in and around Atlantic Avenue. They could all have been deported for lack of credentials, but legalism is slow-moving, and one does not disturb Red Hook unless publicity forces one to.

These creatures attended a tumbledown stone church, used Wednesdays as a dance-hall, which reared its Gothic buttresses near the vilest part of the waterfront. It was nominally Catholic;

but priests throughout Brooklyn denied the place all standing and authenticity, and policemen agreed with them when they listened to the noises it emitted at night. Malone used to fancy he heard terrible cracked bass notes from a hidden organ far underground when the church stood empty and unlighted, whilst all observers dreaded the shrieking and drumming which accompanied the visible services. Suydam, when questioned, said he thought the ritual was some remnant of Nestorian Christianity tinctured with the Shamanism of Thibet. Most of the people, he conjectured, were of Mongoloid stock, originating somewhere in or near Kurdistan—and Malone could not help recalling that Kurdistan is the land of the Yezidis, last survivors of the Persian devil-worshippers. However this may have been, the stir of the Suydam investigation made it certain that these unauthorised newcomers were flooding Red Hook in increasing numbers; entering through some marine conspiracy unreached by revenue officers and harbour police, overrunning Parker Place and rapidly spreading up the hill, and welcomed with curious fraternalism by the other assorted denizens of the region. Their squat figures and characteristic squinting physiognomies, grotesquely combined with flashy American clothing, appeared more and more numerously among the loafers and nomad gangsters of the Borough Hall section; till at length it was deemed necessary to compute their numbers, ascertain their sources and occupations, and find if possible a way to round them up and deliver them to the proper immigration authorities. To this task Malone was assigned by agreement of Federal and city forces, and as he commenced his canvass of Red Hook he felt poised upon the brink of nameless terrors, with the shabby, unkempt figure of Robert Suydam as arch-fiend and adversary.

IV

Police methods are varied and ingenious. Malone, through unostentatious rambles, carefully casual conversations, well-timed offers of hip-pocket liquor, and judicious dialogues with frightened prisoners, learned many isolated facts about the movement whose aspect had become so menacing. The newcomers were indeed Kurds, but of a dialect obscure and puzzling to exact philology. Such of them as worked lived mostly as dock-hands and unlicenced pedlars, though frequently serving in Greek restaurants and tending corner news stands. Most of them, however, had no visible means of support; and were obviously connected with underworld pursuits, of which smuggling and 'bootlegging' were the least indescribable. They had come in steamships, apparently tramp freighters, and had been unloaded by stealth on moonless nights in rowboats which stole under a certain wharf and followed a hidden canal to a secret subterranean pool beneath a house. This wharf, canal, and house Malone could not locate, for the memories of his informants were exceedingly confused, while their speech was to a great extent beyond even the ablest interpreters; nor could he gain any real data on the reasons for their systematic importation. They were reticent about the exact spot from which they had come, and were never sufficiently off guard to reveal the agencies which had sought them out and directed their course. Indeed, they developed something like acute fright when asked the reasons for their presence. Gangsters of other breeds were equally taciturn, and the most that could be gathered was that some god or great priesthood had promised them unheard-of powers and supernatural glories and rulerships in a strange land.

The attendance of both newcomers and old gangsters at Suydam's closely guarded nocturnal meetings was very regular, and the police soon learned that the erstwhile recluse had leased additional flats to accommodate such guests as knew his password; at last occupying three entire houses and permanently harbouring many of his queer companions. He spent but little time now at his Flatbush home, apparently going and coming only to obtain and return books; and his face and manner had attained an appalling pitch of wildness. Malone twice interviewed him, but was each time brusquely repulsed. He knew nothing, he said, of any mysterious plots or movements; and had no idea how the Kurds could have entered or what they wanted. His business was to study undisturbed the folklore of all the immigrants of the district; a business with which policemen had no legitimate concern. Malone mentioned his admiration for Suydam's old brochure on the Kabbalah and other myths, but the old man's softening was only momentary. He sensed an intrusion, and rebuffed his visitor in no uncertain way; till Malone withdrew disgusted, and turned to other channels of information.

What Malone would have unearthed could he have worked continuously on the case, we shall never know. As it was, a stupid conflict between city and Federal authority suspended the investigations for several months, during which the detective was busy with other assignments. But at no time did he lose interest, or fail to stand amazed at what began to happen to Robert Suydam. Just at the time when a wave of kidnappings and disappearances spread its excitement over New York, the unkempt scholar embarked upon a metamorphosis as startling as it was absurd. One day he was seen near Borough Hall with clean-shaved face, well-trimmed hair, and tastefully immaculate attire, and on every day thereafter some obscure improvement was noticed in him. He maintained his new fastidiousness without interruption, added to it an unwonted sparkle of eye and crispness of speech, and began little by little to shed the corpulence which had so long deformed him. Now frequently taken for less than his age, he acquired an elasticity of step and buoyancy of demeanour to match the new tradition, and shewed a curious darkening of the hair which somehow did not suggest dye. As the months passed, he commenced to dress less and less conservatively, and finally astonished his new friends by renovating and redecorating his Flatbush mansion, which he threw open in a series of receptions, summoning all the acquaintances he could remember, and extending a special welcome to the fully forgiven relatives who had so lately sought his restraint. Some attended through curiosity, others through duty; but all were suddenly charmed by the dawning grace and urbanity of the former hermit. He had, he asserted, accomplished most of his allotted work; and having just inherited some property from a half—forgotten European friend, was about to spend his remaining years in a brighter second youth which ease, care, and diet had made possible to him. Less and less was he seen at Red Hook, and more and more did he move in the society to which he was born. Policemen noted a tendency of the gangsters to congregate at the old stone church and dance-hall instead of at the basement flat in Parker Place, though the latter and its recent annexes still overflowed with noxious life.

Then two incidents occurred—wide enough apart, but both of intense interest in the case as Malone envisaged it. One was a quiet announcement in the Eagle of Robert Suydam's engagement to Miss Cornelia Gerritsen of Bayside, a young woman of excellent position, and distantly related to the elderly bridegroom-elect; whilst the other was a raid on the dance-hall church by city police, after a report that the face of a kidnapped child had been seen for a second at one of the basement windows. Malone had participated in this raid, and studied the place with much care when inside. Nothing was found—in fact, the building was entirely deserted when visited—but the sensitive Celt was vaguely disturbed by many things about the interior. There were crudely painted panels he did not like—panels which depicted sacred faces with peculiarly worldly and sardonic expressions, and which occasionally took liberties that even a layman's sense of decorum could scarcely countenance. Then, too, he did not relish the Greek inscription on the wall above the pulpit; an ancient incantation which he had once stumbled upon in Dublin college days, and which read, literally translated,

'O friend and companion of night, thou who rejoicest in the baying of dogs and spilt blood, who wanderest in the midst of shades among the tombs, who longest for blood and bringest terror to mortals, Gorgo, Mormo, look favourably on our sacrifices!'

When he read this he shuddered, and thought vaguely of the cracked bass organ notes he fancied he had heard beneath the church on certain nights. He shuddered again at the rust around the rim of a metal basin which stood on the altar, and paused nervously when his nostrils seemed to detect a curious and ghastly stench from somewhere in the neighbourhood. That organ memory haunted him, and he explored the basement with particular assiduity before he left. The place was very hateful to him; yet after all, were the blasphemous panels and inscriptions more than mere crudities perpetrated by the ignorant?

By the time of Suydam's wedding the kidnapping epidemic had become a popular newspaper scandal. Most of the victims were young children of the lowest classes, but the increasing number of disappearances had worked up a sentiment of the strongest fury. Journals clamoured for action from the police, and once more the Butler Street Station sent its men over Red Hook for clues, discoveries, and criminals. Malone was glad to be on the trail again, and took pride in a raid on one of Suydam's Parker Place houses. There, indeed, no stolen child was found, despite the tales of screams and the red sash picked up in the areaway; but the paintings and rough inscriptions on the peeling walls of most of the rooms, and the primitive chemical laboratory in the attic, all helped to convince the detective that he was on the track of something tremendous. The paintings were appalling—hideous monsters of every shape and size, and parodies on human outlines which cannot be described. The writing was in red, and varied from Arabic to Greek, Roman, and Hebrew letters. Malone could not read much of it, but what he did decipher was portentous and cabbalistic enough. One frequently repeated motto was in a Sort of Hebraised Hellenistic Greek, and suggested the most terrible daemon-evocations of the Alexandrian decadence:

'HEL-HELOYM-SOTHER-EMMANVEL-SABAOTH-AGLA-TETRAGRAMMATON-AGYROS-OTHEOS-ISCHYROS-ATHANATOS-IEHOVA-VA-ADONAI-SADAY-HOMO VSION-MESSIAS-ESCHEREHEYE'

Circles and pentagrams loomed on every hand, and told indubitably of the strange beliefs and aspirations of those who dwelt so squalidly here. In the cellar, however, the strangest thing was found—a pile of genuine gold ingots covered carelessly with a piece of burlap, and bearing upon their shining surfaces the same weird hieroglyphics which also adorned the walls. During the raid the police encountered only a passive resistance from the squinting Orientals that swarmed from every door. Finding nothing relevant, they had to leave all as it was; but the precinct captain wrote Suydam a note advising him to look closely to the character of his tenants and protégés in view of the growing public clamour.

V

Then came the June wedding and the great sensation. Flatbush was gay for the hour about high noon, and pennanted motors thronged the streets near the old Dutch church where an awning stretched from door to highway. No local event ever surpassed the Suydam-Gerritsen nuptials in tone and scale, and the party which escorted bride and groom to the Cunard Pier was, if not exactly the smartest, at least a solid page from the Social Register. At five o'clock adieux were waved, and the ponderous liner edged away from the long pier, slowly turned its nose seaward, discarded its tug, and headed for the widening water spaces that led to old world wonders. By night the outer harbour was cleared, and late passengers watched the stars twinkling above an unpolluted ocean.

Whether the tramp steamer or the scream was first to gain attention, no one can say. Probably they were simultaneous, but it is of no use to calculate. The scream came from the Suydam stateroom, and the sailor who broke down the door could perhaps have told frightful things if he had not forthwith gone completely mad—as it is, he shrieked more loudly than the first victims, and thereafter ran simpering about the vessel till caught and put in irons. The ship's doctor who entered the stateroom and turned on the lights a moment later did not go mad, but told nobody what he saw till afterward, when he corresponded with Malone in Chepachet. It was murder—strangulation—but one need not say that the claw-mark on Mrs. Suydam's throat could not have come from her husband's or any other human hand, or that upon the white wall there flickered for an instant in hateful red a legend which, later copied from memory, seems to have been nothing less than the fearsome Chaldee letters of the word 'LILITH'. One need not mention these things because they vanished so quickly—as for Suydam, one could at least bar others from the room until one knew what to think oneself. The doctor has distinctly assured Malone that he did not see IT. The open porthole, just before he turned on the lights, was clouded for a second with a certain phosphorescence, and for a moment there seemed to echo in the night outside the suggestion of a faint and hellish tittering; but no real outline met the eye. As proof, the doctor points to his continued sanity.

Then the tramp steamer claimed all attention. A boat put off, and a horde of swart, insolent ruffians in officers' dress swarmed aboard the temporarily halted Cunarder. They wanted Suydam or his body—they had known of his trip, and for certain reasons were sure he would die. The captain's deck was almost a pandemonium; for at the instant, between the doctor's report from the stateroom and the demands of the men from the tramp, not even the wisest and gravest seaman could think what to do. Suddenly the leader of the visiting mariners, an Arab with a hatefully negroid mouth, pulled forth a dirty, crumpled paper and handed it to the captain. It was signed by Robert Suydam, and bore the following odd message.

Captain and doctor looked at each other, and the latter whispered something to the former. Finally they nodded rather helplessly and led the way to the Suydam stateroom. The doctor directed the captain's glance away as he unlocked the door and admitted the strange seamen, nor did he breathe easily till they filed out with their burden after an unaccountably long period of preparation. It was wrapped in bedding from the berths, and the doctor was glad that the outlines were not very revealing. Somehow the men got the thing over the side and away to their tramp steamer without uncovering it. The Cunarder started again, and the doctor and a ship's undertaker sought out the

Suydam stateroorn to perform what last services they could. Once more the physician was forced to reticence and even to mendacity, for a hellish thing had happened. When the undertaker asked him why he had drained off all of Mrs. Suydam's blood, he neglected to affirm that he had not done so; nor did he point to the vacant bottle-spaces on the rack, or to the odour in the sink which shewed the hasty disposition of the bottles' original contents. The pockets of those men—if men they were—had bulged damnably when they left the ship. Two hours later, and the world knew by radio all that it ought to know of the horrible affair.

VI

That same June evening, without having heard a word from the sea, Malone was desperately busy among the alleys of Red Hook. A sudden stir seemed to permeate the place, and as if apprised by 'grapevine telegraph' of something singular, the denizens clustered expectantly around the dance-hall church and the houses in Parker Place. Three children had just disappeared—blue-eyed Norwegians from the streets toward Gowanus—and there were rumours of a mob forming among the sturdy Vikings of that section. Malone had for weeks been urging his colleagues to attempt a general cleanup; and at last, moved by conditions more obvious to their common sense than the conjectures of a Dublin dreamer, they had agreed upon a final stroke. The unrest and menace of this evening had been the deciding factor, and just about midnight a raiding party recruited from three stations descended upon Parker Place and its environs. Doors were battered in, stragglers arrested, and candlelighted rooms forced to disgorge unbelievable throngs of mixed foreigners in figured robes, mitres, and other inexplicable devices. Much was lost in the melee, for objects were thrown hastily down unexpected shafts, and betraying odours deadened by the sudden kindling of pungent incense. But spattered blood was everywhere, and Malone shuddered whenever he saw a brazier or altar from which the smoke was still rising.

He wanted to be in several places at once, and decided on Suydam's basement flat only after a messenger had reported the complete emptiness of the dilapidated dance-hall church. The flat, he thought, must hold some clue to a cult of which the occult scholar had so obviously become the centre and leader; and it was with real expectancy that he ransacked the musty rooms, noted their vaguely charnel odour, and examined the curious books, instruments, gold ingots, and glass-stoppered bottles scattered carelessly here and there. Once a lean, black-and-white cat edged between his feet and tripped him, overturning at the same time a beaker half full of a red liquid. The shock was severe, and to this day Malone is not certain of what he saw; but in dreams he still pictures that cat as it scuttled away with certain monstrous alterations and peculiarities. Then came the locked cellar door, and the search for something to break it down. A heavy stool stood near, and its tough seat was more than enough for the antique panels. A crack formed and enlarged, and the whole door gave way—but from the other side; whence poured a howling tumult of ice-cold wind with all the stenches of the bottomless pit, and whence reached a sucking force not of earth or heaven, which, coiling sentiently about the paralysed detective, dragged him through the aperture and down unmeasured spaces filled with whispers and wails, and gusts of mocking laughter.

Of course it was a dream. All the specialists have told him so, and he has nothing to prove the contrary. Indeed, he would rather have it thus; for then the sight of old brick slums and dark foreign faces would not eat so deeply into his soul. But at the time it was all horribly real, and nothing can ever efface the memory of those nighted crypts, those titan arcades, and those half-formed shapes of hell that strode gigantically in silence holding half-eaten things whose still surviving portions screamed for mercy or laughed with madness. Odours of incense and corruption joined in sickening concert, and the black air was alive with the cloudy, semi-visible bulk of shapeless elemental things with eyes. Somewhere dark sticky water was lapping at onyx piers, and once the shivery tinkle of raucous little bells pealed out to greet the insane titter of a naked phosphorescent thing which swam into sight, scrambled ashore, and climbed up to squat leeringly on a carved golden pedestal in the background.

Avenues of limitless night seemed to radiate in every direction, till one might fancy that here lay the root of a contagion destined to sicken and swallow cities, and engulf nations in the foetor of hybrid pestilence. Here cosmic sin had entered, and festered by unhallowed rites had commenced the grinning march of death that was to rot us all to fungous abnormalities too hideous for the grave's holding. Satan here held his Babylonish court, and in the blood of stainless childhood the leprous limbs of phosphorescent Lilith were laved. Incubi and succubae howled praise to Hecate, and headless moon-calves bleated to the Magna Mater. Goats leaped to the sound of thin accursed flutes, and aegipans chased endlessly after misshapen fauns over rocks twisted like swollen toads. Moloch and Ashtaroth were not absent; for in this quintessence of all damnation the bounds of consciousness were let down, and man's fancy lay open to vistas of every realm of horror and every forbidden dimension that evil had power to mould. The world and Nature were helpless against such assaults from unsealed wells of night, nor could any sign or prayer check the Walpurgis-riot of horror which had come when a sage with the hateful key had stumbled on a horde with the locked and brimming coffer of transmitted daemon-lore.

Suddenly a ray of physical light shot through these phantasms, and Malone heard the sound of oars amidst the blasphemies of things that should be dead. A boat with a lantern in its prow darted into sight, made fast to an iron ring in the slimy stone pier, and vomited forth several dark men bearing a long burden swathed in bedding. They took it to the naked phosphorescent thing on the carved golden pedestal, and the thing tittered and pawed at the bedding. Then they unswathed it, and propped upright before the pedestal the gangrenous corpse of a corpulent old man with stubbly beard and unkempt white hair. The phosphorescent thing tittered again, and the men produced bottles from their pockets and anointed its feet with red, whilst they afterward gave the bottles to the thing to drink from.

All at once, from an arcaded avenue leading endlessly away, there came the daemoniac rattle and wheeze of a blasphemous organ, choking and rumbling out the mockeries of hell in a cracked, sardonic bass. In an instant every moving entity was electrified; and forming at once into a ceremonial procession, the nightmare horde slithered away in quest of the sound—goat, satyr, and aegipan, incubus, succubus and lemur, twisted toad and shapeless elemental, dog-faced howler and silent strutter in darkness—all led by the abominable naked phosphorescent thing that had squatted on the carved golden throne, and that now strode insolently bearing in its arms the glassy-eyed corpse of the corpulent old man. The strange dark men danced in the rear, and the whole column skipped and leaped with Dionysiac fury. Malone staggered after them a few steps, delirious and hazy, and doubtful of his place in this or in any world. Then he turned, faltered, and sank down on the cold damp stone, gasping and shivering as the daemon organ croaked on, and the howling and drumming and tinkling of the mad procession grew fainter and fainter.

Vaguely he was conscious of chanted horrors and shocking croakings afar off. Now and then a wail or whine of ceremonial devotion would float to him through the black arcade, whilst eventually there rose the dreadful Greek incantation whose text he had read above the pulpit of that dance-hall church.

As the chant closed, a general shout went up, and hissing sounds nearly drowned the croaking of the cracked bass organ.

Then a gasp as from many throats, and a babel of barked and bleated words—'Lilith, Great Lilith, behold the Bridegroom!' More cries, a clamour of rioting, and the sharp, clicking footfalls of a running figure. The footfalls approached, and Malone raised himself to his elbow to look.

The luminosity of the crypt, lately diminished, had now slightly increased; and in that devil-light there appeared the fleeing form of that which should not flee or feel or breathe—the glassy-eyed, gangrenous corpse of the corpulent old man, now needing no support, but animated by some infernal sorcery of the rite just closed. After it raced the naked, tittering, phosphorescent thing that belonged on the carven pedestal, and still farther behind panted the dark men, and all the dread crew of sentient loathsomenesses. The corpse was gaining on its pursuers, and seemed bent on a definite object, straining with every rotting muscle toward the carved golden pedestal, whose necromantic importance was evidently so great. Another moment and it had reached its goal, whilst the trailing throng laboured on with more frantic speed. But they were too late, for in one final spurt of strength which ripped tendon from tendon and sent its noisome bulk floundering to the floor in a state of jellyish dissolution, the staring corpse which had been Robert Suydam achieved its object and its triumph. The push had been tremendous, but the force had held out; and as the pusher collapsed to a muddy blotch of corruption the pedestal he had pushed tottered, tipped, and finally careened from its onyx base into the thick waters below, sending up a parting gleam of carven gold as it sank heavily to undreamable gulfs of lower Tartarus. In that instant, too, the whole scene of horror faded to nothingness before Malone's eyes; and he fainted amidst a thunderous crash which seemed to blot out all the evil universe.

VII

Malone's dream, experienced in full before he knew of Suydam's death and transfer at sea, was curiously supplemented by some odd realities of the case; though that is no reason why anyone should believe it. The three old houses in Parker Place, doubtless long rotten with decay in its most insidious form, collapsed without visible cause while half the raiders and most of the prisoners were inside; and of both the greater number were instantly killed. Only in the basements and cellars was there much saving of life, and Malone was lucky to have been deep below the house of Robert Suydam. For he really was there, as no one is disposed to deny. They found him unconscious by the edge of a night-black pool, with a grotesquely horrible jumble of decay and bone, identifiable through dental work as the body of Suydam, a few feet away. The case was plain, for it was hither that the smugglers' underground canal led; and the men who took Suydam from the ship had brought him home. They themselves were never found, or at least never identified; and the ship's doctor is not yet satisfied with the simple certitudes of the police.

Suydam was evidently a leader in extensive man-smuggling operations, for the canal to his house was but one of several subterranean channels and tunnels in the neighbourhood. There was a tunnel from this house to a crypt beneath the dance-hall church; a crypt accessible from the church only through a narrow secret passage in the north wall, and in whose chambers some singular and terrible things were discovered. The croaking organ was there, as well as a vast arched chapel with wooden benches and a strangely figured altar. The walls were lined with small cells, in seventeen of which—hideous to relate—solitary prisoners in a state of complete idiocy were found chained, including four mothers with infants of disturbingly strange appearance. These infants died soon after exposure to the light; a circumstance which the doctors thought rather merciful. Nobody but Malone, among those who inspected them, remembered the sombre question of old Delrio: 'An sint unquam daemones incubi et succubae, et an ex tali congressu proles nasci queat?'

Before the canals were filled up they were thoroughly dredged, and yielded forth a sensational array of sawed and split bones of all sizes. The kidnapping epidemic, very clearly, had been traced home; though only two of the surviving prisoners could by any legal thread be connected with it. These men are now in prison, since they failed of conviction as accessories in the actual murders. The carved golden pedestal or throne so often mentioned by Malone as of primary occult importance was never brought to light, though at one place under the Suydam house the canal was observed to sink into a well too deep for dredging. It was choked up at the mouth and cemented over when the cellars of the new houses were made, but Malone often speculates on what lies beneath. The police, satisfied that they had shattered a dangerous gang of maniacs and man-smugglers, turned over to the Federal authorities the unconvicted Kurds, who before their deportation were conclusively found to belong to the Yezidi clan of devil-worshippers. The tramp ship and its crew remain an elusive mystery, though cynical detectives are once more ready to combat its smuggling and rum-running ventures. Malone thinks these detectives shew a sadly limited perspective in their lack of wonder at the myriad unexplainable details, and the suggestive obscurity of the whole case; though he is just as critical of the newspapers, which saw only a morbid sensation and gloated over a minor sadist cult which they might have proclaimed a horror from the universe's very heart. But he is content to rest silent in Chepachet, calming his nervous system and praying that time may gradually transfer his terrible experience from the realm of present reality to that of picturesque and semi-mythical remoteness.

Robert Suydam sleeps beside his bride in Greenwood Cemetery. No funeral was held over the strangely released bones, and relatives are grateful for the swift oblivion which overtook the case as a whole. The scholar's connexion with the Red Hook horrors, indeed, was never emblazoned by legal proof; since his death forestalled the inquiry he would otherwise have faced. His own end is not much mentioned, and the Suydams hope that posterity may recall him only as a gentle recluse who dabbled in harmless magic and folklore.

As for Red Hook—it is always the same. Suydam came and went; a terror gathered and faded; but the evil spirit of darkness and squalor broods on amongst the mongrels in the old brick houses, and prowling bands still parade on unknown errands past windows where lights and twisted faces unaccountably appear and disappear. Age-old horror is a hydra with a thousand heads, and the cults of darkness are rooted in blasphemies deeper than the well of Democritus. The soul of the beast is omnipresent and triumphant, and Red Hook's legions of blear-eyed, pockmarked youths still chant and curse and howl as they file from abyss to abyss, none knows whence or whither, pushed on by blind laws of biology which they may never understand. As of old, more people enter Red Hook than leave it on the landward side, and there are already rumours of new canals running underground to certain centres of traffic in liquor and less mentionable things.

The dance-hall church is now mostly a dance-hall, and queer faces have appeared at night at the windows. Lately a policeman expressed the belief that the filled-up crypt has been dug out again, and for no simply explainable purpose. Who are we to combat poisons older than history and mankind? Apes danced in Asia to those horrors, and the cancer lurks secure and spreading where furtiveness hides in rows of decaying brick.

Malone does not shudder without cause—for only the other day an officer overheard a swarthy squinting hag teaching a small child some whispered patois in the shadow of an areaway. He listened, and thought it very strange when he heard her repeat over and over again.

'O friend and companion of night, thou who rejoicest in the baying of dogs and spilt blood, who wanderest in the midst of shades among the tombs, who longest for blood and bringest terror to mortals, Gorgo, Mormo, look favourably on our sacrifices!'

www.ingramcontent.com/pod-product-compliance
Lightning Source LLC
LaVergne TN
LVHW090619110826
845146LV00001B/450

* 9 7 9 8 8 8 0 9 1 6 4 9 8 *